C

		page

Introduction

'You can't marry me. I like you. I want us to be happy. But in two weeks I'll leave.'

Peter was afraid. Is this a game? he thought. Does she say this to a lot of men? But he knew it was not a game.

When a pretty girl arrives in the small village of Battenbun, Grandpop, Old Pop and Harry Puddleton are very happy. They like pretty girls. Young Peter Puddleton has no time for women because he works hard all the time, but this girl is different. Who is she? Where is she from? Nobody knows, and she won't say. The village women don't like her, and Peter's mother, Rosie, won't have her in the house. But the men of Battenbun are happy that the girl has come to their village.

At the same time a big eel arrives in the river and soon the woods are full of men who want to catch the eel – and the girl!

Catherine Cookson was born in 1906, in Tyneside in the north of England. Most of the books she wrote, like *Slinky Jane*, are about the north. When she was young her family had very little money and she worked hard. Later, she married and went to live in the south of the country. When she was forty years old she began to write books about Tyneside and the north. People from across the world buy these stories. Many of her books – *The Fifteen Streets*, *The Black Velvet Gown* and *The Man who Cried* – are television films and there are plans to film more.

Catherine Cookson wrote more than 90 books. Some of these were for children and some were about her life, but most were stories about the people of Tyneside. She finished her last book in 1997. She died in June 1998.

Chapter 1   A New Girl in the Village

The Puddleton family lived in the village of Battenbun in the north of England. Grandfather – or 'Grandpop', they called him – Puddleton liked to sit in his house and watch the people in the village. There was Grandpop's son, Old Pop, who was seventy-two years old. There was Old Pop's son, Harry Puddleton, and his wife Rosie. Grandpop did not like Rosie – she was always angry with the Puddleton men. They liked to talk and drink and they liked women. Only Peter, Rosie's son, worked hard.

◆

Grandpop Puddleton sat at the window of his old house. I can't walk, he thought, but I can see everything and everybody from here.

◆

One morning an old car stopped at Peter Puddleton's garage in the village.

'Problem, Miss?' Peter asked. The girl in the car was pretty but thin. Her face was very white.

'The car hit something. Can you fix it?'

'I'll try,' Peter said.

'This is a nice village,' said the girl. 'Do you live here?'

'Yes,' Peter replied. 'Our house is the oldest in the village. Puddletons lived here more than two hundred years ago.'

'Your name is Puddleton?'

'Yes, I'm Peter Puddleton. There's my grandfather, Old Pop, his father Grandpop, my mother and father and my two young brothers who are seven years old.'

Harry, Old Pop and Peter's mother, Rosie, walked into the garage. They were very excited.

1

'Problem, Miss?' Peter asked. The girl in the car was pretty and thin. Her face was very white.

'They're going to build a new road through the village,' Harry said. 'The garage is going to be full of cars. We'll be rich!'

'Peter's going to be rich,' Rosie said. 'It's his garage. I bought it for him.'

Harry looked angrily at her. She never wanted him to be happy. She only loved Peter!

Old Pop smiled at the girl. 'Hello, Miss,' he said. Everybody looked at her.

'I'm going to wait at the hotel,' she said. 'Come and tell me when the car's ready.'

The men watched her walk away. She's a pretty girl, Harry thought, and he smiled at her too.

Peter's mother, Rosie, was angry. Why do the Puddleton men like women? she thought. Only my Peter is interested in work, not girls.

But the girls of Battenbun liked Peter. Miss Florrie from the village wanted him. Mavis Mackenzie wanted him too!

◆

In the afternoon Peter looked at the car. I can't fix it today, he thought. It's going to take a long time.

'You took Mavis Mackenzie to town on Saturday night.' Miss Florrie was behind him. She was jealous.

'Yes, I did,' Peter said. 'I told you, Florrie, we can't be friends. You're too young.'

'I'm not too young! I thought you loved me! You're afraid of your mother because she doesn't like me! Mavis wants you because of the garage. Her family want to buy it. You're going to be sorry you took Mavis to town!'

Peter knew she was right. He took Mavis to town because there were no other young women in Battenbun. Now Mavis wanted him and he did not love her.

Chapter 2   Slinky Jane

Peter stopped at Grandpop's house. 'The new road is going through the village,' he said.

'You'll be rich,' Grandpop said. 'Be careful. Those Mackenzies want the garage. They'll try anything to get it from you.'

Grandpop Puddleton did not like the Mackenzies.

◆

Later Peter walked to the hotel. 'Have you come to see that girl?' Mrs Booth, the boss of the hotel asked. 'Who is she?' She was jealous of young pretty women.

Peter did not reply.

'Is the car ready?' the girl asked.

'No,' Peter said. 'It's going to be two weeks.'

'I'll stay here,' the girl said. 'I like this village.' She smiled, but her eyes were sad.

Peter's younger brothers, Jimmy and Johnny, ran into the hotel.

'Quickly, Peter!' Johnny said. 'Come and see! There's a fish – a big eel. It's in the river in the wood.'

'An eel? How big?'

'The biggest! It's bigger than me!' All the Puddleton men liked to fish. The boys were excited; it was a very big eel!

'Let's see,' Peter said. They walked to the river in the wood.

'Look at it,' Johnny said.

Peter looked at the water, then he saw the eel. She was very long. She swam to him. She was beautiful, the most beautiful eel in the world.

'Don't tell anybody,' Peter said to his brothers. 'The men in the village will want to catch her and kill her.'

'Be careful,' Grandpop said. 'Those Mackenzies want the garage.
They'll try anything to get it from you.'

'Is it a fish?' somebody asked. It was the girl.

'Yes, the boys found it,' Peter said.

The girl was next to him. She looked at the river. 'It's an eel!' she said. 'We have eels in my village. She's very big. She's ready to swim to her home in the sea. She's a Slinky Jane.'

'What's a Slinky Jane?' Jimmy asked.

'In my village that's the name for eels,' the girl said.

'We don't want anybody to know she's here,' Peter said.

'I'll stay here and watch her,' the girl said. 'It's quiet here.'

Chapter 3   At the Hotel

The afternoon was very hot. Mavis's brother, Davy Mackenzie, came to the garage.

'We want to buy the garage,' he said. 'You don't get much money from it. We'll give you nine hundred pounds for it.'

'You know the road is going through the village,' Peter said. 'There'll be lots of cars − and a lot of money here. That's why you want the garage. I'm not selling it to you!'

'Think about it,' Davy said, and drove away.

◆

Peter wanted to go home, but Mavis came to the garage.

'Hello,' she said. 'I wanted to see you. Are we going out tonight?'

Peter was afraid. He took Mavis out one night and now she followed him every day. 'No,' he said. 'I'm working.'

'Well!' she said. She was angry and she walked away.

◆

At the house, Rosie asked Peter, 'Who is Slinky Jane?'

'Why?' Peter said.

'I heard your brothers talk about Slinky Jane. Is it somebody in the village?'

'Hello,' Mavis said. 'I wanted to see you. Are we going out tonight?'

Peter smiled.

'Your father isn't here,' Rosie said angrily. 'He's at the hotel.' Peter hated his mother to be angry with his father, but he knew she was right. Harry went to the hotel all the time.

He ate his dinner, washed his face and put on a clean shirt, then he went to the hotel.

He knew Mavis was not there but he saw his father, Harry, with his friend Bill Fountain. The girl with the car was next to them.

'Hello,' she said to Peter.

'Hello, Miss,' he replied. 'How's Slinky Jane?'

She smiled. 'Slinky Jane is OK, thank you. Are you going to see her before it's dark?'

'Yes,' Peter said.

'I'll come with you,' the girl said. Peter looked at her. People in the village always talked about him when they saw him with a girl.

'Thanks for talking to me,' she said to Harry and Bill. She left the hotel. All the men in the hotel watched her. They thought she was pretty and they liked her.

Harry finished his drink. 'I'm going home,' he said. He and Bill left the hotel but they did not go to their houses. They followed the girl to the wood.

Mrs Booth was shocked. 'It's very bad,' she said. 'Harry Puddleton, Bill Fountain and Peter Puddleton all followed that girl into the wood!'

Chapter 4   In the Wood

Peter walked slowly through the wood. I don't want to see Mavis, he thought.

He arrived at the river and looked at the water. The eel was not there. He turned to go home and he heard the girl. Behind her were Harry and Bill.

'Hello, Dad,' Peter said. 'I thought you were at home.'

'I wanted to see the eel,' Harry said.

'Is she here?' the girl asked.

'No,' Peter replied. 'I can't see her.'

'Who found her?' Bill asked.

'My brothers,' Peter replied.

'She's called Slinky Jane,' the girl said.

'That's a good name,' Bill laughed.

'It's late,' Harry said. 'I'm going home. Your mother's going to be angry with me again.'

Bill followed him but Peter stayed with the girl. She was tired and her face was white. Who was she? Where was her home? Where did she plan to go from here? Why was she so tired and sad?

'We won't see Slinky Jane tonight,' she said. 'I'm going back to the hotel.'

◆

They walked through the wood together. It was very quiet. Suddenly she began to laugh.

'What is it?' Peter asked.

'Today . . . the eel, your father and Mr Fountain in the wood . . . all the people in the village . . . they watch me . . .'

Peter heard a sound. 'Quiet,' he said. 'Somebody's coming.'

Four people came through the trees – Mr Collins, his sister Miss Bridget Collins, Mrs Armstrong – and Mavis.

They were shocked when they saw Peter and the girl together in the dark wood.

'Well!' said Mavis. She was angry again and walked quickly away. Peter smiled. Perhaps now she understood he did not love her.

'I can't call you Mr Puddleton. I want to call you Peter.'

'She's unhappy,' the girl said. 'I'm sorry she saw you with me.'

'It's OK,' Peter said. 'She thinks she loves me, but I don't love her.'

The girl laughed again. 'When I came to the village today I thought, I'll never laugh again,' she said.

They walked up the road. 'I'm here for two weeks,' the girl said. 'I can't call you Mr Puddleton. I want to call you Peter.' She was very beautiful.

'What's your name?' Peter asked.

'Call me Leo – Leo Carter.'

'Leo?'

'Yes, short for Leoline.'

'That's an unusual name.'

'Yes, it is.' Suddenly she said, 'I'm going into the hotel now. Don't come with me. Goodnight, Peter. See you tomorrow.'

She smiled her sad smile and he watched her walk to the door of the hotel.

She's going to stay for two weeks, Peter thought.

Something is going to happen.

Chapter 5   A Big Blue Car

It was a difficult morning. Many people from the village came to the garage. His brothers visited him and told him the eel was in the river again.

'We've seen the eel,' Jimmy said, 'but not Miss.'

A car came to the garage, a big blue car. In it were a man and a woman. The man looked at Leo's car.

'Why is that car here?' he asked.

'Somebody wanted me to fix it,' Peter replied.

'I know this car,' the man said. 'The driver – where is she?'

He did not like the man. He watched him get into
the blue car and drive away.

'She's at the hotel,' Peter said.

'I know her,' the man said. 'Miss Carter, isn't it?'

'Yes, it's Miss Carter,' Peter said. He did not like the man. He watched him get into the blue car and drive away. That man knows Leo, he thought. How does he know her? He went to the hotel to find her. 'Is Miss Carter here?' he asked Mrs Booth.

Mrs Booth was not happy. 'Yes, she is. She stayed in bed all morning! Who is she? I want to know.'

'I don't know,' Peter said.

'You don't know?' Mrs Booth asked. 'You're with her all the time!'

Leo came into the room. 'I want to speak to you,' Peter said. 'Let's go outside.' Mrs Booth watched them.

'A man came to the garage,' Peter said. 'He had a big blue car. He says he's your friend.'

Leo's face was shocked.

'Who is he?' Peter asked. 'Is he your husband? Is he coming back?'

'I don't think so,' Leo said, but she did not tell him who the man was.

◆

At three o'clock Rosie came to the garage. She was very angry.

'Where were you last night?' she shouted. 'Were you in the wood with that woman?'

'I went to the wood to look for a – a fish.'

'A fish! Huh! Your father said he went to look for a fish, too – and Bill Fountain. You were with that woman!'

'We were together,' Peter said. 'Dad and Bill and Miss Leo – we all looked for the eel.'

'Now I understand.' Rosie stopped shouting. 'Your brothers talked about an eel in the river.'

'Don't tell anybody. We don't want the men in the village

13

to know about the eel,' Peter said. 'We don't want them to catch her. The girl from the hotel – she watched the eel with us, that's all. Then Mavis saw us and she was jealous.'

'That's good,' Rosie said and smiled. She did not like Mavis because she knew Mavis wanted to marry Peter.

◆

Ten minutes later, Miss Florrie was back in the garage. She asked the same questions as Rosie.

'I heard about you and that girl. You went to the wood last night!'

'*That girl* is Miss Carter,' Peter said. 'Don't talk about her!'

Peter was angry. He liked Leo. Why did the women talk about her behind her back?

He walked down to the river. Old Pop was there.

'I saw her!' Old Pop said. 'The eel! Are we going to catch her?'

'No, leave her,' Peter said.

'I was at the hotel, too,' Old Pop said. 'I saw that girl, Miss Leo. She's a nice girl. She's pretty – and she knows about fish! Do you like her? She's better than Mavis Mackenzie and Miss Florrie.'

Peter laughed. His grandfather was seventy-two and he liked women!

'When I see her I remember a woman – her name was Connie Fitzpatrick. She lived here many years ago. She was a nice girl. The men liked her but the women hated her. They were jealous. They caught her and threw her in the river. They put her in the water. When she tried to climb out they pushed her in again. Grandpop helped her out of the water and took her home. She was very ill, and he stayed with her. That's why he hates the women in the village.

'I think Miss Leo has a problem,' Old Pop said. 'I heard a man talk to her in the hotel but he called her Anna. "Anna,"

'I heard about you and that girl. You went to the wood last night!'
Miss Florrie said.

he said, "you can't stay here. Do you want money?" he asked her. "It's too late for money," she said. "I like the village. I'm going to stay here and watch an eel," she said. What do you think of that, then, Peter?'

Chapter 6   Only Two Weeks

That night Peter went to the wood again. He saw Mavis near the village. 'Where are you going?' she asked.

He did not answer. She began to cry. 'I thought you loved me,' she said.

'Well . . . I don't love you,' Peter said quietly.

'That girl is in the wood,' Mavis shouted. 'Go and find her. All the men want her! You'll be sorry, Peter Puddleton!'

Leo was near the river. She was tired and did not smile when she saw him.

'I saw the eel,' she said. They sat down together under a tree. She was sad.

'Yesterday I was happy here,' she said. 'Now I think I'm going to leave.'

'Why?' Peter asked.

'All these people . . . I like you, Peter. But you think I'm too friendly with the men in the village. Right?'

Peter did not answer her question. 'The man with the blue car,' he said. 'Who is he? Is he your husband?'

'No,' she said. 'He's not my husband. He was my friend. I'm sorry, Peter, I like you but there's something I can't tell you . . . I'm going to leave here tomorrow.'

'I don't want you to leave,' Peter said.

She began to cry. He put his arms round her. His hand was on her hair. He wanted her to stay.

♦

'The man with the blue car.' Peter said.
'Who is he? Is he your husband?'

People in the hotel talked about the girl. Was she Peter's friend? Or Harry Puddleton's? Or Bill Fountain's?

'My wife's angry,' Bill Fountain told Peter. 'Last night, in my sleep, I thought about the eel and I shouted out "Slinky Jane". My wife thought it was that girl's name. I told her it was the eel, but she's very jealous.'

Peter laughed.

Where was Leo? She was not at the hotel. Was she in the village? He looked for her and saw her near the bus stop.

'Let's go down to the river,' she said. 'I want to ask you something.' She was happy again today.

They sat by the water. 'What is it?' Peter asked.

'Can you love me?' Leo said. 'Can you love me for two weeks? Then I'm going to leave the village.'

'I love you,' Peter said. 'But why only for two weeks? No! I want to marry you, Leo.'

'You can't marry me. I like you. I want us to be happy. But in two weeks I'll leave.'

Peter was afraid. Is this a game? he thought. Does she say this to a lot of men? But he knew it was not a game. He pulled her into his arms and kissed her. For a long time they sat next to the river and watched the water.

Chapter 7   Everybody's Talking

Next day, in the village shop, all the women talked about Leo.

'I saw them,' Mrs Booth said to Miss Collins. 'That girl and your brother in the wood. And now she's with Peter Puddleton. Everybody's talking about her.'

'I heard she was with Bill Fountain,' Mrs Armitage said.

'And I saw her with Miss Florrie's father!' Miss Collins said.

'It's very bad,' old Mrs Andrews said. 'She's a bad woman.

When I see her I think of Connie Fitzpatrick – now she was a bad woman too! She liked the men. You remember when we put her in the river?'

Then Miss Florrie came in.

'That woman at the hotel, she likes Peter Puddleton,' Mrs Booth said.

Miss Florrie was angry. 'Do you know where your husband is?' she asked Mrs Booth.

'He's at home.'

'Oh no, he isn't,' Florrie said. 'And do you know where Miss Carter is?'

'She's at the garage with Peter Puddleton.'

'No, she's not, Mrs Booth. I saw her meet your husband. They went into the wood together.' Mrs Booth's face went red and she ran out of the shop. Miss Florrie started to laugh.

◆

Mr Mackenzie came to see Peter.

'I want to buy this garage,' he said.

'Well, I don't want to sell it,' Peter shouted.

'We'll come back another day,' said Mr Mackenzie. 'We'll give you a lot of money for this place.'

◆

At the garage, Rosie was angry. 'Everybody's talking about you and that girl, Peter.'

'Be quiet!' Peter shouted.

Rosie was shocked. Peter never shouted. 'Don't shout at me,' she said. 'I'm your mother.'

'Well, be careful when you talk about Miss Carter!'

Rosie did not stop. 'She's a bad woman. Are you taking her to the games today?' she asked.

'Yes, I am,' Peter said.

For a minute Rosie was quiet, then she turned and walked out of the garage. It was the first time Peter shouted at her and she was afraid. He did not listen to her now that Leo was in the village.

Peter was unhappy. He loved his mother, he never shouted at her. But Leo was important. I know she's going to leave when I fix her car, he thought, but I love her. I don't know her, but I want to marry her.

◆

Every year there was a games day in Battenbun and Peter was always first in the five-mile run. Before the run started, he went to the wood. He saw Mavis and Miss Florrie. That's unusual, he thought, Miss Florrie always says she hates Mavis.

At the river he found Leo. He sat next to her and kissed her. 'Is the eel here?' he asked.

'No, not today,' Leo said. 'It's going to rain. When it rains Slinky Jane will leave, you know. I want to see her again.'

Peter did not come first in the five-mile run. People laughed at him. 'It's because of that girl,' they said. 'He can't run because he loves that girl.'

Peter looked for Leo. 'Were you first?' she asked when he found her.

'No,' he said. 'But it's not important.'

They walked together through the village. He saw Miss Florrie again. Her face was red and she was angry. She hates me, Peter thought.

The sky was dark. 'It's going to rain,' Peter said.

'I like the rain,' Leo said. They walked slowly. It started to rain and soon they were very wet.

'Come on,' Peter said. He took Leo's hand and began to run. Her face turned very white. Then she fell.

'Leo! What is it? Are you ill?'

She did not answer. Her eyes were closed. He wanted somebody to help. A car came along the road. The driver was Miss Florrie. She saw them but she did not stop.

*Peter carried Leo along the road. After two or three minutes
she began to move.*

Peter carried Leo along the road. After two or three minutes she began to move.

'Are you OK?' he asked.

'Yes,' she said quietly. They were near the hotel.

'Are you ill, Leo?' Peter asked.

'No, I'm OK,' she said.

Peter was afraid. There was something wrong.

Chapter 8   A Fight – and Some Answers

At nine o'clock Peter went back to the hotel. The big blue car was outside. The driver was in the hotel.

'Hello,' he said to Peter. 'I want to talk to you.'

Peter sat next to him. 'What is it?'

'You and Anna,' the man said. 'I'm going to tell you something. Stay away from Anna.'

Who was this man? Why did he call Leo 'Anna'? 'Why?' Peter asked. 'Are you her husband?'

'No, I'm not her husband. But we lived together. You'll only be unhappy with her.'

Before he spoke again, four young men came into the hotel. They laughed and made a lot of noise. Peter looked at them. One man was very tall and had brown hair. The other men called him Tiffy. Another was small; his name was Roger.

'Come on, Tiffy,' Roger said. 'Sing to us.'

'OK,' Tiffy said and began to sing. He was a beautiful singer. For a minute Peter forgot the man with the blue car and listened to Tiffy sing.

Suddenly Tiffy stopped. He looked at the door. 'Look!' he said. 'It's Leo!'

She was near the door. The man ran to her. 'Leo!' the small man said. 'Leo! My love!'

Before he spoke again, four young men came into the hotel. They laughed and made a lot of noise.

'Hello, Roger,' Leo said to him. Then she saw the man with the blue car next to Peter. She was shocked. Peter was angry. Did Leo know *every* man in the world? He forgot she was ill after the race. He forgot that he loved her.

'Come on, give me a little kiss, Leo!' Tiffy said.

'Stop it, Tiffy,' Roger said, but Tiffy did not listen. He put his arm round Leo. 'Come on, just one little kiss.'

Peter stood up and took Tiffy's arm to stop him kissing Leo.

'Who are you?' Tiffy asked. He laughed. 'Are you a friend of Leo's? I'm a friend of Leo's, too. We're *all* friends of Leo's.'

Peter tried to hit him. 'You want to fight?' Tiffy said. He was not laughing now. 'OK, we'll fight.' He pushed his friends away.

'Stop it!' Leo shouted.

'Yes, stop it,' the man with the blue car said.

Harry and Bill Fountain were in the hotel. They tried to stop Peter but Peter was too angry and jealous. He tried to hit Tiffy again.

'Get out of my hotel!' Mrs Booth shouted. 'I'll call the police!' She saw Leo. 'You! This is you! Get out of here, you dirty –'

The men went outside and Peter fought Tiffy in the street. Soon all the men started to fight. Somebody hit Bill and he fell down. The man with the blue car tried to hit Peter but Harry went to stop him . . . After five minutes they all stopped. Peter was hurt.

'Are you OK?' Roger asked. 'I'm sorry this happened. Tiffy likes Leo. He helped her.'

Peter was angry again. 'All the men like Leo,' he said.

'You don't understand,' Roger said. 'We're doctors. We were Leo's doctors. She's ill – did you know that?'

'Ill?' Peter asked. 'How?'

'Sit down and listen to me,' Roger said. 'You love her. Am I right?'

'Yes, I do.'

Peter was angry and jealous. He tried to hit Tiffy again.

'I'm going to tell you something. Leo was in our hospital but we can't help her. She's going to die. She left the hospital four months ago in her old car. We didn't know where she was. We all like her very much. She's a good woman.'

Peter began to cry. He loved Leo. He wanted to marry her. She must not die!

'Care for her,' Roger said. 'Stay with her.'

Peter turned to his father. 'Where's Leo?' he asked.

'In the hotel,' Harry said. 'She's afraid.'

'And the man with the blue car? Where's he?'

'He's gone,' Harry said. 'He ran away.'

Peter went into the hotel. 'This isn't right!' Mrs Booth shouted. 'Fighting in my hotel. You and that woman. She's –'

'Shut your mouth,' Peter said quietly. He took Leo's arm and they walked slowly into the street. 'I'm taking you home,' Peter said.

Harry saw his son's face and said nothing, but he thought, Rosie is going to kill him!

◆

He was right. When they got to the house, Rosie looked at Leo. 'That woman's not coming in here!' she shouted.

'You be quiet,' Harry said. 'Leave her.'

Rosie was shocked. Harry never usually told her what to do! She turned and looked at Peter and the girl. She was jealous. Her Peter and that woman . . .

'I'm sorry, Mrs Puddleton,' Leo said quietly. 'I'm not going to stay here.'

'Come on,' Peter said. 'You must sleep.'

Not in my house, Rosie thought. She watched Peter take the girl up to the bedroom. She opened her mouth to speak but Grandpop stopped her. 'Be quiet!' he said. He turned to Leo. 'You go to bed, Miss. Nobody's going to hurt you in this house.'

'Leave them,' Harry said to Rosie. 'You don't like her, but Peter loves her. He's a man now, you know, not your little boy!'

◆

Soon Peter came down again. 'Listen to me,' he said. 'Leo's very ill. She's going to die. I'm taking her away from here. I'm going to care for her.' He began to cry. Rosie looked at him. My son, my Peter, is going to leave, she thought. How can I stop him?

Chapter 9   Peter Makes Plans

The family sat at the kitchen table. 'I'm leaving Battenbun,' Peter said. 'I'll sell the garage to the Mackenzies. They always wanted it.'

'But Leo's ill. She must stay here,' Rosie said.

'We can't. This village –' Peter didn't finish. Rosie knew he was right. The women in the village hated Leo because the men liked her too much. Rosie began to cry and went into the kitchen.

◆

Harry, Old Pop and Grandpop were shocked. 'You can't sell the garage to the Mackenzies!' Harry said. 'What about the new road? What about all the money when the cars come through Battenbun on the new road?'

'It's not important,' Peter said. 'I must care for Leo.'

Leo came into the room. She was very white and cold.

'I told you to stay in bed,' Peter said.

'I want to talk to your mother. I must talk to her.'

'Talk to her tomorrow,' Peter said.

'No. If I can't talk to her now, I'm going back to the hotel.'

'Listen,' Peter said. 'We're going to leave here together.

'He left his wife and lived with me. I had a baby but it died.
I was ill and Arthur left me.'

Nothing will stop me. I love you.' He took her out of the room.

'You're different,' Leo said. 'Why don't you ask questions? Do you know I'm ill? Did Tiffy and Roger tell you about the hospital?'

'Yes, so we're going to stay together. I'm going to care for you.' He put his hand on her hair. 'Don't cry, Leo.'

'There's very little time. I'm tired, I can't fight. But I must tell you – I love you.' Leo closed her eyes. 'Your mother's angry,' she said. 'She doesn't want you to leave with me.'

'She knows I love you,' Peter said.

'Oh, Peter.' Leo's voice was quiet. 'I must tell you . . . Arthur, the man with the blue car –'

'I don't want to know,' Peter said.

'I *want* you to know. I lived with him for one year. He sold cars – I met him at a garage. He loved me, but he had a wife. He left her and lived with me.' She looked at her hands. 'I had a baby but it died. I was ill and Arthur left me. He went back to his wife. Roger and Tiffy – they're doctors. They cared for me.'

'It's finished,' Peter said. 'Forget Arthur. I'm going to care for you now. Go to bed. I'll send my mother up to you in the bedroom.'

He went to the kitchen. 'Mother,' he said to Rosie. 'Please do something for me. Go and talk to Leo. She wants you.'

◆

Peter left the house and went to see the Mackenzies.

'I want to sell the garage,' he said to old Mr Mackenzie. 'I know you want it. You can have it, but I must sell it now.'

Mr Mackenzie was very happy. The new road is going to bring lots of cars to the garage, he thought. He gave Peter more than one thousand pounds for the garage.

Chapter 10 Dangerous Women

The next day was Sunday. The streets in the village were quiet because everybody was in church.

Mrs Booth talked to Miss Florrie. 'It was very bad,' she said. 'Those four young men wanted to kiss that girl – and she liked it! And Peter Puddleton tried to stop them – he's with her all the time. Then they all started to fight in the street –'

'Remember Connie Fitzpatrick?' old Mrs Andrews said. 'She wanted all the men so we threw her in the river. That stopped her!'

'That Miss Leo is a bad woman,' Miss Collins said.

'Peter Puddleton wants to marry her,' Mavis said.

'Marry her – then she'll stay here! No! We must stop him,' Mrs Booth said. 'I told you she was bad. She goes into the wood with our men. They say they're looking for the eel – but no women can see this eel, only her! I don't think there *is* an eel!'

'Throw her in the river,' old Mrs Andrews said. 'That's the best thing to do. She'll leave us then.'

◆

Grandpop was unhappy. Peter's leaving, he thought. I don't want him to go. And the girl. I like the girl. Leo came into the room. 'Grandpop,' she said. 'I'm going down to the river. I want to see the eel again. She's going to leave soon.'

'Yes, she's going to leave soon. Go and see her. But be careful – don't go through the village. Stay away from those women.'

'Yes,' Leo said sadly, 'I'll stay away from them.'

For a minute Grandpop slept in his chair. Suddenly Jimmy and Johnny ran into the house. 'Grandpop!' they shouted. 'Grandpop!'

For a minute Grandpop slept in his chair. Suddenly Jimmy and Johnny ran into the house.

'I will – I must,' Grandpop said. Jimmy looked at him. He was
very old and his legs were slow, but he climbed out of his chair and
left the house.

'Stop shouting,' Grandpop said. 'What is it?'

'We saw the women in the village . . . Miss Collins, Miss Florrie, Mrs Booth and Mrs Andrews . . . they want to throw Miss Leo in the river! We heard them. They say she's going in the water three times, then she'll leave Battenbun.'

'Is she going to die, Grandpop?' Johnny asked. 'Are they going to kill her?'

'No,' Grandpop said. 'We must stop them.'

'But you can't walk,' Jimmy said.

'I will – I must,' Grandpop said. Jimmy looked at him. He was very old and his legs were slow, but he climbed out of his chair and left the house.

'Johnny,' he said, 'find Old Pop and bring him to the wood.'

Slowly Grandpop and Jimmy walked to the river.

'We must get Leo away from the wood and stop those women,' Grandpop said. 'Jimmy, run down to the river. Find Leo and tell her I'm here. But be quiet. The women must not see you!'

Jimmy ran quickly to the wood. It was dark in the trees, but across the river he saw Leo.

Chapter 11   Leo and Slinky Jane

Leo sat by the water. I'm going to die, she thought, but before I die, Peter and I are going to be happy together for a time.

She looked for Slinky Jane in the water. Then she saw somebody through the trees. It was the girl who liked Peter – Miss Florrie. Next to her were Mrs Booth, Mrs Andrews and Miss Collins. Mrs Booth's eyes were hard and angry. She hates me, Leo thought. She wants me to die. What can I do? They're going to kill me!

The women came quickly through the trees. Leo looked at

the river again. The water was cold and deep. I can't swim, she thought, and I can't run away.

'Oh Peter, Peter!' she said quietly.

Then she heard a noise and saw Jimmy across the river.

'Swim,' he shouted.

'I can't,' she said. 'The water's too deep.' But she knew she must move fast.

The women were behind her. I'm going to die, she thought. The women or the river will kill me!

Leo climbed into the river. The water was cold. It went over her legs, her arms, her head!

'Come on, Miss!' Jimmy said.

'I can't.' Her head went under again.

'You must! It's not far. Grandpop's waiting for you.' The little boy began to cry.

Then something happened. The eel came under her and pushed her quickly across the water to Jimmy. One minute she was under the water; the next minute she was near Jimmy!

He pulled her out of the water. 'Quickly, Miss,' he said.

'Let's go. Grandpop is going to help you.' He took her hand.

'Grandpop! But he can't walk,' Leo said.

'He's here, Miss.'

Slowly they walked through the wood. Grandpop saw her.

'Oh Leo,' he said. 'What are those women trying to do to you? This is very bad.'

'I'm afraid,' Leo said. 'Very afraid. I can hear them. They're coming! They want to kill me.'

'Don't be afraid,' Grandpop said. 'I'll see about those women. They won't hurt you. Jimmy, take Leo home.'

◆

Grandpop sat near a tree and waited.

The women came through the wood and saw him. They stopped. 'You go back,' he shouted, 'or I'll call the police!'

Miss Florrie and Miss Collins were afraid but Mrs Booth was angry.

'Move!' she shouted. 'We want that woman.'

'I can't move,' Grandpop said. 'I can't walk. Come near me and I'll hit you!'

The women were shocked. 'You're a bad old man,' Mrs Booth said. 'Let me find that woman.'

'You leave her! You're a bad woman, Katie Booth! You want to hurt Leo because the men like her. I know you! You're all jealous! You want the men but *they* don't want *you*. And you,' he shouted at Mrs Andrews, 'you're the same as her!'

He stopped. He was very tired. Are they going to leave? he thought.

He saw Miss Florrie begin to walk away and slowly the women followed her. Only Mrs Booth stayed.

Then Old Pop arrived. 'What happened?' he asked. 'Why is Grandpop on the floor? You hit him, Katie Booth?'

'Hit him? He's a bad old man! All you Puddletons are bad . . .' Mrs Booth turned and ran away too.

Old Pop looked at Grandpop. 'How did you get here?' he asked. 'You can't walk!'

'I can walk when I must,' Grandpop said. 'Now help me to get home.'

Chapter 12   Leaving Battenbun

Peter took Leo's hand. 'I'll kill them!' he said. Leo was wet and cold. 'Are you OK?' he asked. 'We'll take you home.'

'No,' Leo said. 'I can't go back to the village.'

'You *must* come home,' Rosie said. She was sad and angry. She saw Mrs Booth and the women and she knew they were wrong. Leo was not a bad girl. She was young and pretty and

Slowly Leo put out her hand and Rosie took it. Leo kissed her and got into the car.

the men liked her, but she was not a bad girl. And Peter loved her – that was the most important thing. Now Rosie wanted to help her. 'A day or two in bed –'

'No,' Leo said. 'I'm going to leave.'

'She's right,' Harry said. 'Let them go.'

'But the garage . . .' she said.

'The Mackenzies can have the garage,' Harry said.

Rosie was shocked. Yesterday Harry was angry because Peter wanted to sell the garage to the Mackenzies. Today he was not angry about it, he was happy. Grandpop and Old Pop were happy too . . . Rosie did not quite understand.

'I'm leaving with you. I'm going to stay with you always now,' Peter said to Leo. 'We're going together.' Peter went for the car. He drove through the quiet village. There was nobody in the streets.

Rosie took Leo's arm. 'Get in the car,' she said. 'Put this coat on to keep you warm.' She was friendly and motherly now.

◆

Peter looked at his family. He loved them but he loved Leo more and Leo must leave the village.

Harry took his arm. 'You go, son. When you're – when Leo isn't there, come back to Battenbun. This is your home.'

'Perhaps,' Peter said. 'One day. But not for many years.'

'Leo's a good woman,' Grandpop said. 'Be happy.'

'Let's go,' Peter said to Leo.

Leo stood with the three Puddleton men. Jimmy and Johnny took her hands. 'Don't forget us,' Harry said.

Leo kissed Grandpop. 'We'll see you again,' he said. 'I know we'll see you again.'

Rosie was next to Peter. Leo looked at her. Slowly she put out her hand and Rosie took it. 'I always wanted a daughter,' Rosie said quietly. Leo kissed her and got into the car.

'Thanks, Mother,' Peter said.

'OK,' Rosie said. 'Go now. Perhaps I'll come and see you one day.'

'I'll write to you, Mother,' Peter said and slowly he drove the car out of Battenbun.

The men watched them go, and they heard Rosie begin to cry. Rosie *never* cried!

Harry took her arm. 'I'm here, girl,' he said. 'Come on, it's OK. Peter'll come home when Leo is –' he stopped. Then he laughed.

'I have something to tell you,' he said. 'About the garage.'

Grandpop began to laugh too. 'Tell her!' he said. 'Tell her!'

'You know the Mackenzies gave Peter a lot of money for the garage because the new road is coming through the village?' Harry said.

'Yes,' Rosie said. She did not want to think about the garage.

'Well, there's going to be a new road,' Harry said, 'but it's not coming through Battenbun!'

Rosie began to laugh. 'So the Mackenzies got nothing,' she said. 'I'm happy to hear that!'

'Hey! I can't walk!' Grandpop said loudly. 'Carry me home!'

And all the Puddletons laughed together. It was the first time Rosie laughed with the men.

'I'll carry you, Grandpop,' Harry said.

'Carry me slowly. When we walk through the village I want to tell Katie Booth what I think of her,' Grandpop said.

'That's a good idea,' Rosie said. 'You can't go to the hotel – she won't let you in. So we'll walk *very* slowly through the village.'

Grandpop smiled. 'You're right, Rosie,' he said. 'For the first time, I think you're right.'

ACTIVITIES

Chapters 1–4

Before you read

1　Look at the pictures in this book. Do you think the story happens in the present time? Why or why not?

2　This book is called *Slinky Jane*. What does *slinky* mean? Look in your dictionary. Who do you think Slinky Jane is?

3　Look up these words in your dictionary and then answer the questions.

　eel   fix   jealous   reply   shocked

　Make sentences using these words:

　a　eel/river/swim

　b　friend/jealous/computer

　c　fix/television/picture

4　Finish these sentences:

　a　Susan's sister has a lot more friends than she has, and Susan is very ..... of her.

　b　Anna's grandmother is ..... by Anna's short skirts.

　c　'Where are you going?' Paul asked.

　　　'To the cinema,' Jim ......

　d　'My camera isn't taking very good photos. Perhaps they can ..... it at the shop in town.'

After you read

5　Answer these questions about the Puddleton family.

　a　Who is the oldest person in the family – Grandpop or Old Pop?

　b　What is the name of Old Pop's son?

　c　What are the names of Peter's mother and father?

　d　What are the names of Peter's brothers?

6　Why is the girl going to stay in the village?

7　Why do the Mackenzies want to buy the garage?

8 Two of the village girls are interested in Peter. Who are they?

Chapters 5–8

Before you read

9 Find these words in your dictionary:
   care for kiss
   Which word or words could you find in a story about:
   a hospitals?
   b love?
10 Why do you think Leo is so sad?
11 Leo says that people in the village are watching her. Why do you think this is?
12 What do you think will happen to the eel?

After you read

13 Why doesn't Rosie like Mavis?
14 Who was Connie Fitzpatrick and what happened to her?
15 Why is Bill Fountain's wife angry with him?
16 Who asks these questions? Who answers?
   a 'Are we going to catch her?'
   b 'But why only for two weeks?'
   c 'Do you know where your husband is?'
   d 'Are you taking her to the games today?'
   e 'Were you first?'
17 Who drives past Peter and Leo?
18 Who is the man in the blue car?
19 Why does Peter fight Tiffy?
20 What does Roger tell Peter about Leo and the men?

Chapters 9–12

Before you read

21 Find the word *deep* in your dictionary
   Make a sentence using these words:
   deep/river/swim

22 Do you think Rosie can stop Peter? How?

23 What do you think will happen to the garage?

After you read

24 How much does Peter get for the garage?

25 How does the Slinky Jane help Leo?

26 Why does Rosie say the Mackenzies got nothing when they bought the garage?

27 Find the right second half for each sentence a–d:

    a Peter wants to sell the garage to the Mackenzies .....

    b The village women want to throw Leo in the river .....

    c Leo doesn't want to climb into the river .....

    d Rosie is sad and angry .....

    ..... because she can't swim.

    ..... because he's leaving Battenbun.

    ..... because she knows the village women are wrong.

    ..... because then she'll leave the village.

Writing

28 Write what you think happens to Peter and Leo after they leave Battenbun.

29 Write two or three sentences about each of the Puddleton family.

30 You are Rosie. Write a letter to Peter and Leo telling them what happens in the village after they leave.

31 A year later Peter comes back to Battenbun and he talks to Rosie about his future plans. Write their conversation.